Lion Practice

Emma
Carlisle

Macmillan
Children's
Books

My name is
Laura and I
love to practise.

I love kangaroo practice,

boing boing boing!

parrot practice,

flap flap flap!

and elephant practice too.

whoooosh!

And I'm VERY good at crocodile practice.
Everyone thinks so.

Mum says that today I should practise being something small and quiet, like a mouse.

But I have a much better idea. Today I will try...

Lion practice!

Lions walk on their
hands and feet, like this...

And lions
have the
messiest
manes,
like this...

PERFECT!
But what else?

I think lions
are good
at hiding,

and
leaping,

and running VERY fast!

Oh, and I know,
lions roar REALLY
loudly, like this...

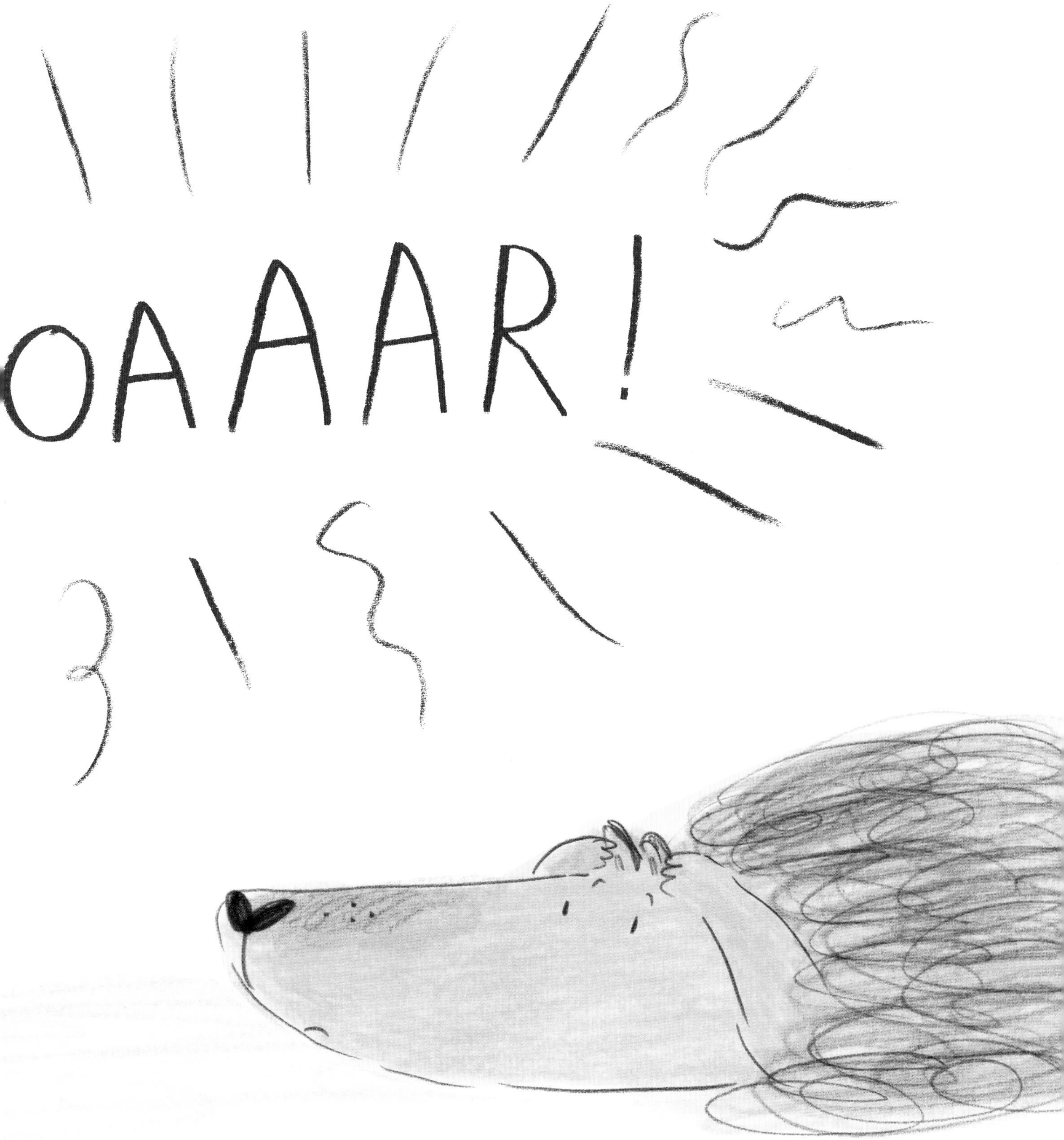
OAAAR!

But mum and dad didn't
like my roaring,
or my leaping.
They told me to
stop running
around and
keep the
noise down.

"oh dear...

I'm sorry...

I just...

... I just wanted to
be a good lion."

Dad came out
and found me...

...and then mum came too.

"Don't be sad, Laura", they said.

"Guess what we've
been practising?"

A little lion?

A little LION!

What else do
little lions do?

Mum says they need
a BIG dinner.

And dad says they need extra
bubbles at bath time.

I say little lions
don't like pyjamas.

Mum and dad
say I can be a cheeky
monkey sometimes...

A cheeky monkey?
That sounds like fun!

I'm going to practise being
one of those tomorrow.